THE CHILDREN'S STORY OF
MUSIC & PAINTING

Anthea Peppin and Simon Mundy

Illustrated by Joseph McEwan

Designed by Graham Round and Kim Blundell

Edited by Robyn Gee

Consultant Editor: Dr Anne Millard

First published in 1980 by Usborne Publishing Ltd,
20 Garrick Street, London WC2E 9BJ. Copyright © 1980
Usborne Publishing Ltd.
Published in the U.S.A. in 1980 by Hayes Books,
4235 South Memorial Drive, Tulsa, Oklahoma, U.S.A.
Published in Canada by Hayes Publishing Ltd, Burlington,
Ontario.
Published in Australia by Rigby Publishing Ltd,
Adelaide, Sydney, Melbourne, Brisbane.
Printed in Belgium by Henri Proost & Cie pvba, Turnhout.
Typesetting by F. J. Milner & Sons, Brentford, England.

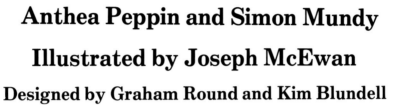

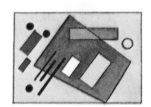

Cave Paintings

No-one knows when the story of painting really began. The earliest paintings that we know about were done about 30,000 years ago, in the Old Stone Age. They are on walls, deep inside caves. People probably painted on other things, such as bark and skin as well, but no evidence for such paintings survives.

We can only guess at why people began to paint pictures, but it seems likely that they did them for magical or religious reasons.

Hunting magic

Most prehistoric cave paintings show large animals such as horses, mammoths and bison, like the one above. Some of the best-preserved and most famous ones are at Altamira in Spain and Lascaux in France.

Most of the paintings are in deep caves. They often show arrows or spears pointing at the animals. It seems likely that they were painted because of hunting magic, rather than to provide decoration.

How cave paintings were done

Brush made of animal hair tied to a small bone

The paint is stored in hollow bones with lumps of fat in the ends

Lamp made by burning fur or moss soaked in animal fat

Grinding coloured rocks between a stone and a bone

In 1940 some very famous cave paintings were found at Lascaux, in France. Some boys were taking their dog for a walk. It disappeared and they eventually found it in the cave.

FRANCE

• Lascaux

• Altamira

SPAIN

Prehistoric people had to make their own paints. They ground up certain coloured earths to make reddish, brown and yellow pigments. They mixed this powder with blood, fat, egg white or plant juice to make a kind of paint, which they put on the walls with brushes made of animal fur or feathers and pads made of moss or leaves.

Egyptian Paintings

1

In Ancient Egypt art was closely linked with religion. The Egyptians believed that when people died they went to live in another world. In order for this to happen the dead body had to be preserved as a mummy. It was dried, wrapped in cloth and put in a painted case.

2

The tombs of dead people were decorated with paintings. These showed the life they had lived on earth, and the kind of life they were expecting in the next world.

4

This tomb painting shows a harvest scene. Important people were always painted larger than their servants and slaves.

3

Special spells written on scrolls in hieroglyphs (picture writing) and illustrated with paintings have been found inside coffins. These are known as the Book of the Dead.

5

Although the remains of the temples and palaces built by the Ancient Egyptians are now mostly bare stone, they, too, were once decorated with paintings.

A different way of drawing

1

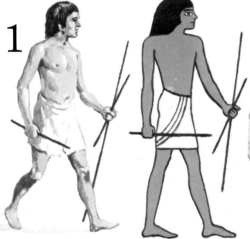

Modern view   Egyptian view

Egyptian painters showed things in a way that seems strange to us. In pictures of the human body, the head, arms and legs were shown from the side but the body and eyes are seen

2

from the front. In the picture above, the ducks, fish and trees are all shown from the side but the pond is shown from above. The things they painted are not very real-looking, but

3

all the parts of the picture they thought important are shown more clearly than you would be able to see them in real life. For them, the purpose was to record things.

Painting in the Ancient World

The art of the Ancient Greeks and Romans is called Classical art. When the Romans took over the Greek Empire they were strongly influenced by Greek sculpture and painting, and the Classical style has continued to influence European artists ever since.

Greek vases

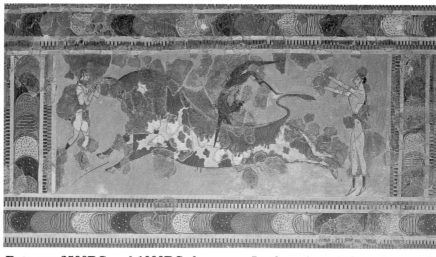

Between 2500BC and 1000BC there were people living on the island of Crete who were very skilled artists.

In the ruins of the palace at Knossos, many wall paintings, like the one above, have been found.

Later vases have red figures on a black background.

Early vases have black figures on a red background.

The Etruscans

The Etruscans were the ancient inhabitants of central Italy, who were later conquered by the Romans. They admired Greek art and imported many Greek vases and statues. They also admired and copied Greek painting. Some of their paintings, done on the walls and ceilings of tombs cut into rocks, have survived. This one of musicians dates from about 480BC.

We know from ancient writings that the Ancient Greeks covered their walls with paintings, but most of these have disappeared. Many painted vases have survived, however, and these show us what Greek painting was like. On early vases the figures are rather awkward looking, but on later ones they are more life-like.

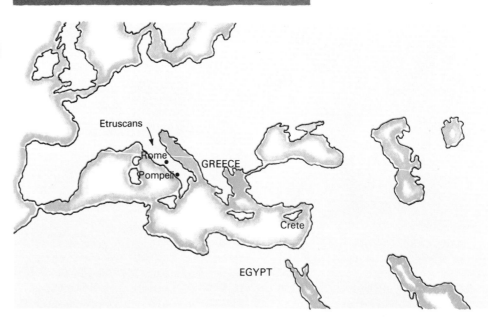

4

Roman paintings

When the Romans conquered the Greeks, Roman collectors brought Greek works of art to Rome. These were copied by Roman artists. The copies that survive are mainly statues made of marble and bronze.

In AD79 Mount Vesuvius, a volcano in Italy, erupted and buried the town of Pompeii and other nearby towns in hot ash and lava. Many houses and villas in these towns had paintings on their walls.

When archaeologists excavated the houses they found that some of these paintings had been preserved.

Some Roman wall paintings show graceful figures, like this girl picking flowers.

Views of buildings and landscapes made the rooms they were in seem bigger.

Portraits painted in the Roman style have been found on Egyptian mummy cases.

Early Christians

The first Christians in the Roman Empire worshipped in secret. In Rome they often used underground tomb passages called catacombs. The pictures found on catacomb walls show people from Bible stories.

The paintings of the early Christian artists are very clear and simple and the people look rather stiff. This is because they were more interested in telling a story than in painting realistically. This picture shows Jesus Christ as the Good Shepherd.

The Middle Ages

In the 4th century AD, Christianity was established as the official religion of the Roman Empire. From this time onwards, the Christian religion had a strong influence on all forms of art.

In the 5th century AD the Roman Empire in the west was overrun by barbarian tribes, and, for a time, art and learning continued only in the monasteries. The eastern (Byzantine) part of the Roman Empire survived and there painting continued as before.

Holy images

1

Artists in the Byzantine Empire painted pictures of saints and holy people. These are called icons (images). They show unreal figures against gold backgrounds.

2

In the 8th century a group of people who disapproved of icons gained power. They destroyed all those they could find. They were called iconclasts (image-breakers).

1 Art and learning in the monasteries

Between the 5th and 12th centuries Christian monks were the most important artists in Europe.

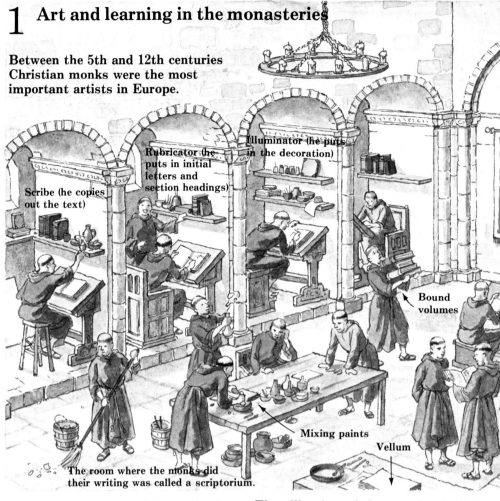

Scribe (he copies out the text)

Rubricator (he puts in initial letters and section headings)

Illuminator (he puts in the decoration)

Bound volumes

Mixing paints

Vellum

The room where the monks did their writing was called a scriptorium.

Monks copied out the Bible and other religious books by hand on to a specially fine type of parchment (animal skin) called vellum. Most of the writing was in Latin.

They illuminated the margins, initial letters and sometimes whole pages with pictures and decorations. Illuminating one book may well have taken a monk his whole life.

2

3

These pages are from the Lindisfarne Gospels, a book made around 700AD by monks on the island of Lindisfarne, off the north of England. The decoration is so elaborate that it probably took the artist several days to complete one square centimetre. On the left is a full-page decoration; on the right a decorated initial (first letter of a new section).

Gold leaf

Gold can be beaten into sheets so thin that you can see through it. It used to be stuck on paintings or illuminated manuscripts. Sometimes it had a pattern pressed into it.

Frescoes

A fresco is a painting done on damp plaster. It dries very quickly so the painter must work fast. Mistakes cannot be corrected. If dry plaster is used the paint will peel off later.

1 Giotto

The Italian artist, Giotto, (AD1267/1337) became famous for doing paintings that looked much more real than other paintings of this time.

2

He was employed to paint wooden altarpieces and frescoes on the walls of churches in Florence (his home town), and several other Italian cities.

3

His frescoes in the Arena Chapel in Padua tell stories from the life of Christ. He tried to show what people were feeling instead of using them as decoration. These people are mourning because Jesus is dead.

4

No shading   Shading

Giotto tried to make his people life-like by using shading to make them look solid.

Pictures in churches

In Western Europe people argued about whether to allow pictures in churches. In the 6th century Pope Gregory the Great declared that paintings were useful for teaching and reminding people about the Bible. After this it became usual to have pictures in churches.

Pictures to stand on the altar were painted on wooden panels. They are often in three sections, like the one above. This is called a triptych.

Originally sculptures, like this one, were often painted in bright colours.

Sculptures carved from stone, showed saints and stories from the Bible.

Stained glass windows often show Bible stories as well as patterns.

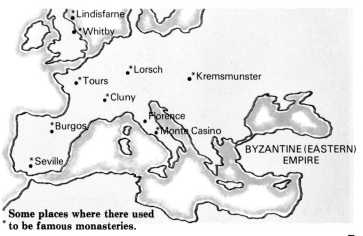

Some places where there used to be famous monasteries.

7

The Early Renaissance

In Italy in the early 15th century, people began to take a great interest in art and learning. Artists started experimenting and asking questions instead of following the style established by tradition. Painters began to paint more and more realistically. They became specially interested in the works of art created in Ancient Greece and Rome, so the time became known as the Renaissance, which means rebirth or revival.

This fresco, by an artist called Masaccio (AD1401/1428) is on the wall of a church in Florence. It shows Christ with his disciples, and St Peter paying the tax collector. Masaccio's figures look solid, every face had its own character and each person has room in which to move. At that time, this way of painting was considered startlingly different.

What is perspective?

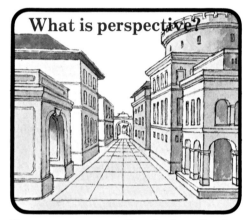

For many years artists had realized that to make things appear far away, you have to draw them smaller. In Florence in the 15th century a set of rules was worked out so that this could be done scientifically. We call this system perspective. When it is used to paint people they look much more solid and real, as in Masaccio's painting.

How paints were made

Powdered colours (pigments)

Fresh egg yolk

Pestle and mortar for mixing paint

Water (mixed with egg yolk)

Until recently there were no ready-made paints; painters had to mix their own. In the 15th century Italian painters used a paint called tempera. Here are the ingredients.

Using the ideas of the Ancient World

Italian artists looked at things made by the Greeks and Romans for inspiration. Painted portraits became popular. They were often done in profile (side view) like the portrait heads on Roman coins.

Artists also began to use stories and characters from the myths and history of Ancient Greece and Rome in their paintings. Here are Venus (goddess of love) and Mars (god of war) by the artist Sandro Botticelli (AD1445/1510). Botticelli is probably the most famous painter of the Early Renaissance. Several of his most famous paintings were done for the Medici family.

1 Becoming a painter

To become a painter a boy had to become "apprenticed" to a master in a workshop. There he learned to make paint, clean brushes and palettes and to draw.

After he had served as an apprentice for several years he might become an assistant. He would put in outlines and paint the background and some of the details.

Eventually he might become the master of a workshop. The master did the main bits of the painting. He belonged to a guild which licensed him to sell paintings.

1 Producing a painting

Artists did not just produce any painting they felt like and then hope to sell it to someone. Most paintings were specially commissioned by a noble, a churchman, a merchant or some other wealthy man. The master would probably have gone to see this "patron" to find out what kind of painting he wanted and see where the painting was to hang.

Then the patron had a contract drawn up. This stated the size, subject and price of the painting. Sometimes it also laid down the number of figures and the colours.

Back in the studio the master planned the painting, the apprentices prepared the materials and the assistants started work. The more the patron had agreed to pay, the more painting the master actually did himself. At the end he would check the whole picture to make sure he was satisfied with the standard of work.

A famous patron

This is Lorenzo de Medici, the head of the most important family in Florence during the 15th and 16th centuries. The Medici were famous for their patronage of art, architecture and learning.

Painting in Northern Europe

At the time that the Renaissance was starting in Italy, artists in the north of Europe were painting in a very different way. Their paintings were full of detail and jewel-like colours. Italian ideas spread to the north later.

In the 16th century changes in religious thinking led artists in Northern Europe to produce many more non-religious paintings.

In the 15th century, the cities of Tournai, Ghent and Bruges in Flanders were great centres of the wool trade and of weaving and making tapestries.

This meant that, besides the aristocrats, many people of the merchant class now had money to spend on such luxuries as paintings.

Oil paints

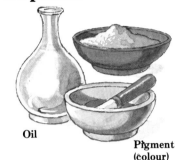

Oil

Pigment (colour)

While Italian artists were still using tempera, artists in Flanders were using oils. Oil paint dries much more slowly, so artists can work more carefully and in much greater detail. It also gives richer colours.

A master of detail

A painter of nightmares

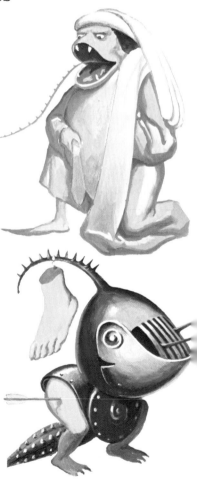

Portraits were popular in Northern Europe. This double one is by Jan van Eyck. Notice all the details he has put into it—the slippers, the fruit, the dog's hair. In the mirror at the back of the room you can see the whole scene reflected from behind.

Many of the paintings by Jerome Bosch are crammed with strange details. This is what he imagined hell to look like.

These are some of the weird and ugly creatures from his painting of hell enlarged so that you can see them more clearly.

10

Italian ideas spread to Northern Europe

Making an engraving.

Printing copies.

This is the German, Albrecht Dürer, doing a self-portrait. Dürer, had travelled to Italy. He was impressed by Italian ideas and wanted to spread them to other artists.

One way of spreading ideas was to make engravings of paintings and print lots of copies. As well as being a great painter, Dürer was one of the first great engravers.

Dürer was always experimenting with ways of painting things more realistically. Here he is looking at his model through a pane of glass and painting what he sees.

Portraits for a king

Hans Holbein the Younger (his father was also an artist) was another German who knew about Italian art. He went to England and worked for Henry VIII.

Henry VIII was so impressed by Holbein's paintings that he gave him the official title of court painter. His main job was to paint pictures of the members of the royal household, so most of his paintings are portraits. He also designed jewellery, decorations for halls and costumes for pageants.

Henry was thinking of marrying Ann of Cleves, but he had never met her. He sent Holbein to do this portrait of her, so he could see if she was pretty.

Everyday scenes

Pieter Bruegel, a Flemish painter, is famous for his pictures of everyday life, like this one of children playing. He painted ordinary, often ugly, people at work or enjoying life.

Famous artists

The Netherlands

AD1378/1444   Robert Campin
AD1390/1441   Jan van Eyck
AD1399/1462   Rogier van der Weyden
AD1440/1482   Hugo van der Goes
AD1435/1494   Hans Memling
AD1450/1516   Jerome Bosch
AD1525/1569   Pieter Bruegel

Germany

AD1460/1528   Mathis Grünewald
AD1471/1528   Albrecht Dürer
AD1473/1553   Lucas Cranach (the elder)
AD1489/1538   Albrecht Altdorfer

This map shows the area known as Flanders. It was the southern part of the "Netherlands" or "Low Countries" and is roughly the same as modern Belgium and Luxembourg.

11

The High Renaissance

The period between about AD1500 and about AD1527 in Italy is called the High Renaissance because people feel that this was the time of greatest artistic achievement. Rome replaced Florence as the most important centre for artists, and the Popes became the leading patrons in Italy.

Three artists stood out above all the rest. They were Leonardo da Vinci (AD1452/1519), Michelangelo (AD1475/1564) and Raphael (AD1483/1520).

Mona Lisa

This is Leonardo's most famous painting. It is the portrait of a Florentine lady and is called the Mona Lisa. It is painted in soft colours, as though everything is seen through a slight haze. The blurring of outlines, which gives this effect, is called *sfumato*. The lady's skin glows and the shadows on her face are very soft. The strange landscape behind adds to the air of mystery given by her slight smile. There is a story that Leonardo hired musicians to keep her amused while he painted.

Leonardo da Vinci

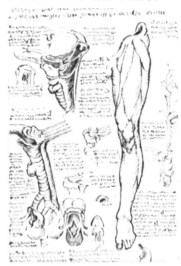

Amazing records of Leonardo's work survive in his notebooks full of sketches and notes written in mirror writing.

He also studied the human body by cutting up corpses. Eventually the Pope forbade him to do this.

He made sketches of the bodies he cut up. This is a drawing of an unborn baby.

He had many interests besides painting. He studied nature in a way that no one had done before and he was also a most original inventor. Here he is in his room, studying plants and insects that he has collected.

Leonardo was interested in so many things that he did not always finish what he began. He left many unfinished paintings. This is a design or "cartoon" for a painting he never did. It shows the Virgin Mary, Jesus, St Anne and St John the Baptist. Only about 15 finished paintings by him survive.

Michelangelo

Experts now think that Michelangelo was probably standing up, rather than lying down, when he painted the ceiling of the Sistine Chapel.

Michelangelo was a sculptor, an architect and a painter. His best known painting is the fresco on the ceiling of the Sistine Chapel in the Vatican in Rome. On it he showed scenes from the Bible and numerous other figures. It was an enormous work and he did it all by himself. It took him four years to do. He had to work on scaffolding and he found that painting over his head was a great strain.

Raphael

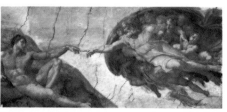

This is a detail from the Sistine Chapel. It shows God creating Adam. The figures almost give the impression of being sculptures.

Plato   Heraclitus

The painter Raphael was in Rome at the same time as Michelangelo. They knew each other but did not get on well together, although they admired each other's work. Raphael was also working for the Pope. He painted some small rooms (known as Stanze) in the Vatican. One of these shows the "School of Athens". In it Raphael has imagined what the Ancient Greek scholars and thinkers would have looked like.

In the "School of Athens" the figure representing the philosopher Plato is thought to be a portrait of Leonardo, while Heraclitus may well be a portrait of Michelangelo.

13

Late Renaissance and Mannerism

People thought that the art of the High Renaissance was so perfect that it was very difficult for young painters of the next generation to find ways of improving on the past. Some of them reacted by breaking the rules of Renaissance painting, and distorting the figures and space in their pictures. This often looks very dramatic. We call this style Mannerism.

In the 16th century young artists studied hard to learn from Michelangelo's paintings, particularly the ones he did towards the end of his life. These contain lots of nudes in complicated positions, like these ones from his picture of the Last Judgement, painted on the altar wall of the Sistine Chapel.

Some painters chose to exaggerate certain parts of the body to achieve a particular effect. This picture by Parmigianino is called "The Madonna of the Long Neck". Other parts of Mary's body, besides her neck, have been elongated to make her look graceful. Artists also made the space in their pictures look strange. Notice how small the man in the right corner is, and how the angels are crammed together on the other side of the picture.

An early art historian

The artist Giorgio Vasari travelled all over Italy, finding out about artists and works of art. He used this information to write a book about the history of art. It was published in 1550. Much of what we know about early artists comes from this book.

Famous artists

Mannerists

AD1494/1556	Jacopo Pontormo
AD1503/1540	Francesco Parmigianino
AD1503/1572	Agnolo Bronzino
AD1511/1574	Giorgio Vasari

Venetians

AD1430/1516	Giovanni Bellini
AD1478/1510	Giorgione (Giorgio del Castelfranco)
AD1490/1576	Titian (Tiziano Vecellio)
AD1518/1594	Jacopo Tintoretto
AD1528/1588	Paolo Veronese

Painters in Venice

Not all the Italian artists in the later 16th century were Mannerists. In Venice, which was rather isolated and different from the rest of Italy, artists had developed their own style or "school". Venetian artists, like those of the High Renaissance, were specially interested in colour and light.

Most of the famous Venetian artists painted altarpieces. Some of these large canvas paintings are still standing in Venetian churches.

Painting on canvas

At about this time, canvas began to be widely used instead of wooden panels. Canvas has to be stretched and coated with size (a type of glue) before you can paint on it.

Cleaning old paintings

Canvas rots with age, especially if it is allowed to get too damp or too dry. Nowadays picture restorers can preserve old paintings by transferring them to a new piece of canvas.

Friend of kings and emperors

The most brilliant and famous of all the Venetian artists was Titian. All the most important men of his day, from the Pope and Emperor downwards, were eager to have their pictures painted by him. He helped to make full-length portraits fashionable. This portrait of the Emperor Charles V, was done in 1530 and is one of the first of its type. Titian became a personal friend of Charles V, which, in those days, was an unheard of honour for an artist.

15

Baroque Painting

In the 17th century a style of art known as Baroque developed. It was especially well suited to large scale pictures—the kind of painting you would expect to find in a church or palace. There was most demand for works like this in Roman Catholic countries such as Italy, Flanders and Spain.

Painted ceilings were very fashionable at this time. The artists painted stone structures so cleverly, that from the ground they look real. The figures are also painted as though seen from below and appear to be floating through the air. This effect is known as "illusionism".

The paintings of Caravaggio influenced painters all over Europe. He used strong contrasts of light and shadow to make his paintings more exciting. He often made the people and objects in his pictures seem to burst out of the frame. In the one above, Jesus (in the middle) has just surprised his companions. The hand of one and the elbow of another seem to come out of the picture at you.

Studying ruins in Rome

The centre of Baroque art was Rome. Artists from all over Europe came to find out about the latest styles and fashions, and to study the great works of Ancient Rome and the High Renaissance. Many, like Caravaggio, Carracci, Claude and Poussin, made their homes there.

Classical landscapes

Two French artists, Claude Lorraine and Nicolas Poussin, spent most of their working lives in Rome. Many of their paintings show the hills and plains around Rome. This type of painting is known as a "classical landscape". The figures are tiny, Roman ruins are often included, and the colours are soft greens, blues and browns.

A busy studio master

Grid to help assistants transfer ideas from Rubens' sketches on to canvas.

Rubens brought the fashion of using huge canvases with him from Italy.

The Flemish painter, Peter Paul Rubens, worked in Italy as a young man. He learnt a great deal there. When he returned to Flanders his work was in such demand that he employed other artists to work in his studio and had teams of pupils and assistants. Often he did very little of a painting himself, but supervised each stage of the work.

Rubens was often used as a diplomat by his patrons, who included the rulers of France, Spain, England and Flanders. Here he presents Charles I of England with a painting from the King of Spain, who wanted peace with England.

At the Spanish court

Many of Rubens' paintings are on big canvases and are full of life. He developed a very dramatic, free way of painting, using big, energetic figures. This painting is called "The Battle of the Amazons".

In Spain, the most famous painter of this time was Diego Velazquez. He worked at court and painted many portraits of the king and his family. This one is of the young princess Margarita and Velazquez in his studio.

17

The Great Century of Dutch Painting

Holland became an independent, Protestant country during the 17th century. Before this it had been ruled by Spain as the northern part of Spanish Netherlands. The new Dutch Republic quickly became a rich and powerful trading nation.

Paintings were immensely popular in 17th century Holland. The demand was so great that many artists had to specialize in doing a particular type of painting, in order to reach a higher standard.

In Roman Catholic countries the Church had always bought a lot of paintings, but Protestants did not approve of religious paintings and Dutch churches were kept very plain.

The new capital city, Amsterdam, became a bustling centre of trade. The merchants who profited from this trade wanted to buy paintings of themselves and their interests.

Popular subjects for painters

Dutch merchants loved to have their portraits painted, either by themselves or in groups. Some of the best-known of these portraits are by the artist, Frans Hals.

Holland also had a prosperous farming community and another popular subject for painters was domestic animals such as cows, sheep and poultry.

Pictures of everyday scenes, like this one, are known as "genre" paintings. Dutch ones show tidy, comfortable rooms in private houses.

Some Dutch painters specialized in pictures of carefully arranged objects, like fruit, flowers, jugs and dishes. These are called "still-life" paintings.

Landscape artists painted views of the flat Dutch countryside, dotted with trees, windmills and churches. They became very skilled at painting large areas of sky.

Holland's wealth was founded on her sea trade, so it was natural that pictures of ships and the sea would be popular. These also showed great expanses of sky.

A Dutch market

Many artists painted pictures before they had found people to buy them. Before this nearly all pictures were specially ordered by a buyer. Artists sold their paintings at markets and fairs. There was strong competition and it was hard to make a living. Many painters had to do other jobs besides painting.

A number of people started making a living as picture dealers. They bought pictures from artists and sold them at a profit. The artist Vermeer was himself an art dealer.

Rembrandt

Rembrandt is the most famous of all Dutch painters. This is one of over 70 portraits that he did of himself throughout his life. It shows him as a young man.

Rembrandt was a great collector. He bought old-fashioned costumes, armour and weapons at auctions and kept them in his studio so he could paint them into his pictures.

In the early part of his career Rembrandt was a highly successful portrait painter. His most famous painting, "The Nightwatch", is a group portrait of a company of guardsmen in Amsterdam. It is not a formal painting, but even included dogs and children. Each person posed separately for this painting and the figures look quite relaxed.

Later, Rembrandt started to paint, not to please wealthy clients, but just to please himself. He painted stories from the Bible and from ancient history, but he could not always sell them. Despite this, he was extravagant. He spent far more money than he earned and got into debt. His wife and son died and his last years were spent in poverty and loneliness, but he continued to paint.

Rococo and Neoclassical Painting

In the early 18th century, Paris took the place of Rome as the centre of the arts. There a new style called Rococo* developed. Also at this time, excavations at and near Pompeii in Italy, brought to light more classical works of art. This stimulated a new interest in the Ancient World and gave rise to the Neoclassical (new classical) style.

These two styles—Rococo, on this page, and Neoclassical on the facing page—are in strong contrast to each other.

After the death of King Louis XIV in AD1715, French noblemen moved from his grand place at Versailles back to Paris. There they built elegant town houses, which they decorated in the new Rococo style. This room, with its large windows and mirrors, intricate carvings and delicate colours, is typical of this style.

Rococo paintings are usually of cheerful subjects, like well-fed, well-dressed people, enjoying picnics and parties out of doors. They are light and colourful and show the sort of lives French aristocrats wanted to live. This fairyland, where everything is pleasant and peaceful, contrasted strongly with the poverty-stricken lives led by most ordinary people. The most famous painter of this kind of picture was Jean-Antoine Watteau.

In this famous painting by Jean-Honoré Fragonard, the girl on the swing kicks off her shoes while the young man blushes at the glimpse he gets of her legs.

Exhibitions

In the 18th century so many people became interested in art that many societies for the exhibition of paintings were formed. Later some of these became public galleries.

Collectors

Rich connoisseurs built up private collections. They were visited by artists and gentlemen doing the "Grand Tour" of Europe, as part of their education.

*This comes from the French word *rocaille*, which means "rock-work".

◄This room is in the Neoclassical style. Neoclassical architecture, interior design and painting is very plain and simple if you compare it with Rococo.

▼ Artists painted in the style they thought the Ancient Romans would have used and often chose classical subjects. Jacques-Louis David, a Frenchman who had visited Rome, was the most famous Neoclassical painter. The picture below, called "The Oath of the Horatii", shows three young men swearing to fight to the death with the enemies of Rome.

England

Most English patrons only wanted to buy portraits, but some English artists were able to combine these with other subjects they found more interesting. Thomas Gainsborough often set his figures in light, feathery landscapes.

Sir Joshua Reynolds sometimes dressed his subjects as characters from ancient history and myths.

Academies

Academies were founded in most European capital cities. They held exhibitions and ran schools of painting, which taught strict rules about how to paint properly.

Famous artists

Neoclassical

AD1748/1825   Jacques-Louis David

England

AD1697/1764   William Hogarth
AD1723/1792   Sir Joshua Reynolds
AD1727/1788   Thomas Gainsborough

Rococo

AD1684/1721   Jean-Antoine Watteau
AD1703/1770   François Boucher
AD1732/1806   Jean-Honoré Fragonard

William Hogarth did series of paintings which tell stories. Here a young couple are forced to marry by their greedy fathers. Five scenes later the story ends in disaster.

Romantics and Realists

In the early 19th century a new way of thinking gave rise to a style in painting, literature and music, which is called Romantic.

Romantic artists thought that showing feelings and emotions was more important than anything else. They were inspired by the idea of liberty and by anything mysterious, exciting or exotic and they often looked to history and nature for their subjects. They tended to use strong colours and dramatic effects in their paintings. This type of painting was very different from the Neoclassical style, which many painters still followed and which was taught in the academies.

Another style of painting, which arose at this time, was Realism. Realist painters were reacting against the use of imaginary and idealized subjects. They wanted to paint the world exactly as they saw it, so they chose poor people in everyday situations as their subjects.

Many painters gained their inspiration from writers. The poet, Lord Byron, shown above was one of the great romantic heroes of this age.

This "Mounted Officer of the Guard" is much more than a portrait. Filled with excitement and violent energy, it shows the life of one of Napoleon's soldiers, probably not as it actually was but as the artist, Théodore Géricault, liked to imagine it to be. Géricault loved drama and heroic deeds. He painted this picture when he was 21. He was soon to become a leading figure among French Romantic painters.

The most famous Romantic painter, Eugène Delacroix, loved exotic subjects. "The Death of Sardanapalus", which you can see above, was inspired by the story of the luxury-loving king of Ancient Assyria.

The Spaniard, Francisco de Goya, produced many paintings that show his hatred of the war he saw around him in Spain. Here, he shows Napoleon's troops executing citizens of Madrid.

Nature and Romantic painters

Landscape painting played an important part in the Romantic movement. A favourite theme was to show the power of nature

Towering mountains, storms and rough seas make men seem weak and defenceless.

This painting of a train, by the English painter, Turner, is called "Rain, Steam, Speed". Turner tried to convey a feeling of being present at a scene, rather than showing what it actually looked like. He did many watercolours as well as oil paintings.

John Constable's paintings give a realistic view of the English countryside. Most of them are of places in Suffolk, where he grew up. "The Haywain", (above), is probably his most famous painting.

Famous artists

Romantics

AD1746/1828   Francisco de Goya
AD1775/1851   Joseph Mallord William Turner
AD1776/1837   John Constable
AD1791/1824   Théodore Géricault
AD1798/1863   Eugène Delacroix

Realists

AD1819/1877   Gustave Courbet

Watercolours

Watercolours had been used earlier but they became especially popular in England at this time. The paint is diluted with water so that light from the paper shows through.

Painting poor people

Some French artists felt that it was time to stop painting from imagination. They observed and painted peasants and labourers—people whose lives were hard and unromantic and became known as "Realists".

"The Stonebreakers" by Gustave Courbet caused an uproar when it was first shown. Critics felt that this was an unworthy subject (It was destroyed during World War II and only photographs of it survive).

Impressionists and Post-Impressionists

The group of painters known as the Impressionists came together as students in Paris during the 1860s. The movement was at its height during the 1870s and continued into the 1880s. The Impressionists were more interested in conveying atmosphere, through their use of light and colour, than in the subject matter of their paintings. The period that followed this involved a variety of different styles, which all come under the description of Post-Impressionist. This just means "after the Impressionists".

1

2

This painting may not seem very shocking today, but in 1863, when it was painted, it caused a scandal. People said it was rude and badly painted.

It was painted by Edouard Manet. People were so shocked by his paintings that he was not allowed to show them in the "Salons" (the official exhibitions of the French Royal Academy).

Edouard Manet. People were so shocked by his paintings that he was not often allowed to show them in the "Salons" (the official exhibitions of the French Royal Academy).

(shown above) by Claude Monet. One art critic called the group "Impressionists", because of this painting. He was being rude, but soon they adopted the name for themselves.

Painting out of doors

The Impressionists were interested in light. They painted mainly in the open air and avoided using black, which you rarely see in nature; their shadows are made up of many colours.

Claude Monet painted mainly outside. Sometimes he painted the same place at different times of the day or year to show the effects of changing light on the same scene.

Café life

Many Impressionist paintings show Paris, or places nearby. Some show everyday scenes of people enjoying themselves. Life in the cafés was a favourite subject.

Famous artists

Impressionists

AD1830/1903   Camille Pissaro
AD1832/1883   Edouard Manet
AD1834/1917   Edgar Degas
AD1839/1899   Alfred Sisley
AD1840/1926   Claude Monet
AD1841/1919   Pierre-Auguste Renoir

Post-Impressionists

AD1839/1906   Paul Cézanne
AD1848/1903   Paul Gauguin
AD1853/1890   Vincent van Gogh
AD1859/1891   Georges Seurat
AD1864/1901   Henri de Toulouse-Lautrec

Photographs and painting

The invention of photography had a great influence on painting. Many people felt that now that a machine could produce accurate pictures of the real world, there was no point in painters doing the same thing.

2

When portable cameras were invented, photographs, taken from odd angles, could capture, unposed actions, like someone doing up their shoe. Painters like Edgar Degas started painting this type of scene.

Japanese prints

During the later 19th century, many Japanese prints were sent to Europe as wrapping paper for other goods. This totally different style of art made a deep impression on many painters.

After the Impressionists

1

After moving to Paris in 1886, the Dutch painter, Vincent van Gogh. was strongly influenced by both Impressionist paintings and by the Japanese prints he saw there.

2

He painted everyday subjects in brilliant colours, which he used so thickly that they look as though they have been squeezed straight out of a tube onto the canvas.

3

Paul Cézanne used the Impressionists' discoveries about light and colour, but painted more solid objects. He often changed their shape, to make the picture as a whole look right.

4

5

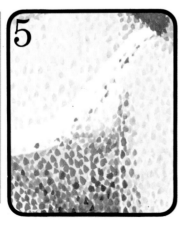

To paint this picture, "The Lady with the Powder Puff", Georges Seurat used a method called pointillism (using lots of small dots).

He studied the science of colour and realized that if you paint lots of small dots next to each other, they mix in your eye.

6

This painting by Paul Gauguin is of native women on the island of Tahiti in the South Pacific. Gauguin went to Tahiti in search of simple people and a simple life. The paintings he did there are his best works. He used clear outlines and large patches of flat colour, rather like stained glass windows.

Modern Painting

In the 20th century, many artists have stopped painting recognizable objects. They use colours and shapes to express their ideas and feelings. This kind of painting is usually called "Abstract".

Other painters are still concerned with "representing" real objects, but they use new methods and new subjects. On this page you can see different types of Abstract painting, and on the facing page, Representational painting.

1

2

The round blobs are probably the fruit.

The shape of the neck and head of a guitar can be seen on the left of the picture.

The tall black shape looks like the neck of a bottle with a cork in the top.

Notice the guitar strings going across the sound hole in the centre.

The Spanish painter, Pablo Picasso, and his friend Georges Braque, developed a new style of painting. They chose objects, imagined them to be made up of geometric shapes, and painted them as though seen from many different angles. This style of painting is called Cubism. The painting above is called "Fruit Dish, Bottle and Guitar".

One style that grew out of Post-Impressionism was Expressionism. One Expressionist group worked in Paris. They liked violent colours and often changed the shape of the things they painted. Because of this they became known as the "Fauves" (wild beasts). This picture is by their leader, Henri Matisse. It shows his friend, the artist, André Derain.

3

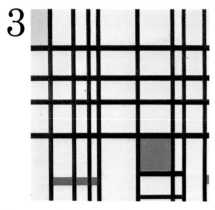

Action Painting

Some artists took the idea of painting in geometric shapes a stage further than the Cubists had done. Piet Mondrian used only straight lines and primary colours.

In the 1940s New York became an important centre for painters. One group, the Action Painters, felt that the way an artist paints is just as important as the picture he creates.

The artist, Jackson Pollock, made his pictures by dribbling paint onto huge canvases laid out on the floor. Others painted large canvases in a single colour.

26

Painting dreams and fantasies

In the 1920s a style of art called Surrealism appeared. Surrealists painted objects realistically, but combined them in an unusual or nonsensical way. They felt that such odd combinations would stir up ideas and feelings in the backs of people's minds. These paintings often have a dream-like quality. This one by René Magritte is called "Time Transfixed".

Using photographs

The artist David Hockney used small drawings and many black and white and coloured photographs to help him paint this couple in their home.

In paintings like this he gives a realistic record of people and places he knows. This is one of a series of double portraits of his friends.

A very recent development is to project photographs on to canvas and then copy them exactly. Funnily enough, paintings like this, often have a beauty that was not in the photograph.

Famous artists

AD1869/1954	Henri Matisse
AD1872/1944	Piet Mondrian
AD1881/1973	Pablo Picasso
AD1898/1967	Rene Magritte
AD1912/1956	Jackson Pollock
AD1923/	Roy Lichtenstein
AD1937/	David Hockney

Pop Art

Since World War II, there has been a move to make art deal with the ordinary world, by painting things that are common in city life. This is called Pop Art.

This painting by Roy Lichtenstein is based on a comic strip. Artists working in this style do not copy directly, but make many changes in size, shape and colour to get the result they want. They seem to want us to look at and enjoy the world around us in a new, fresh way.

Painting in India

In India, religion has always played an important part in the lives of the people and much of its great art has been produced in the service of religion.

The Hindu religion grew up with the beginning of civilisation in India. Buddhism began in about 600BC, and spread to other countries in the East. Islam, the religion of the Muslims, was brought to India from the Middle East, by Muslim warriors. The most famous Muslim invaders were the Moguls, who, in the 16th century, set up an empire in northern India.

Paintings for Muslim rulers

Some of the finest Indian paintings are the book illustrations produced at the court of the Mogul emperors. The Moguls were immensely rich and great patrons of the arts. Miniature paintings, like the one above, were done in brilliant colours and show great detail. A painting was often produced by a team of artists working together.

Buddhist painting

When the Buddha (Prince Gautama, who founded Buddhism) is represented in sculptures or paintings, he always has certain key features, as shown above.

The Moguls brought the art of painting miniatures with them from Persia. Persian miniatures, like the one above are more decorative than Mogul ones.

Mogul paintings show scenes from life in the palaces of the princes and emperors, and portraits of the rulers and their families, rather than religious scenes.

The row of Buddhas, shown above, is in a cave at Ajanta, a Buddhist holy place. Some of the oldest paintings in India are in caves cut into the rocks.

Mogul painting had a great influence throughout India. Hindu painters began to use this style to paint religious scenes. The Hindu god, Krishna, usually shown with blue skin, was a favourite subject.

Painting in the Far East

As in other parts of the world, painting in the Far East was strongly influenced by religious beliefs, particularly Buddhism and Taoism. Painters aimed at simplicity and stillness in their pictures. The oldest Chinese paintings that survive were painted nearly 2,000 years ago.

For the Chinese, calligraphy (the art of handwriting) was as important an art as painting. A piece of calligraphy was often hung on a wall like a painting, and many paintings have writing on them.

Paintings were often done on scrolls. These could be either hanging scrolls or hand scrolls. Hand scrolls could be up to 30m long. They were kept on rollers and unrolled and viewed section by section.

Painters' materials

Ink Brushes Paper Watercolours

Chinese artists used either ink or watercolours, which they applied with soft brushes with bamboo handles. They painted on either silk or paper.

Chinese artists painted a wide range of subjects, but many of their best paintings are landscapes, like the one above. They painted with incredible speed, but they thought a great deal about the painting before they began, and knew exactly what they were going to do. Once they had begun they could not make any changes.

Japan

In Japan coloured prints, made by using carved blocks of wood, became very popular in the 18th and 19th centuries. Many of the best artists were employed by the publishers of these prints. Their designs were first done on paper, then cut into woodblocks by engravers and printed in their hundreds. They often showed scenes from everyday life, like the fishing scene on the right.

Primitive Art

The term, Primitive Art, is used to describe the art of peoples who have not been influenced by the great centres of civilisation. This includes paintings done by the Eskimos, the Indians of North and South America, Africans and the Aborigines of Australia.

Buffalo hide painted by North American Indians.

Painted totem pole by Eskimos in Canada.

Painted mask from Sri Lanka.

Painted African mask.

Rock painting by African tribes in the Sahara Desert.

Body painting by Indians near the River Amazon, South America.

Bark painting by Australian Aborigines.

Primitive Art, though very different from the art of the developed world, is not necessarily backward. Much of it is extremely sophisticated and skilfully produced. Like the cave paintings done in the Old Stone Age, it often has a magical or superstitious purpose. In the 20th century the art of these isolated peoples has exercised a great influence on many artists in Europe and America.

Paul Gauguin was one of the first European artists to look to the art of isolated peoples for inspiration and ideas. He went to live on the island of Tahiti in the South Pacific.

Some 20th century artists, like Picasso, became excited when they discovered African masks. Primitive carving and sculpture has influenced them more than primitive painting.

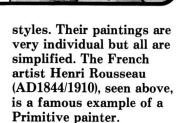

Some painters in the developed countries of the world, produce what are known as Primitive paintings. They, like the primitive peoples, are isolated—they are not influenced by traditional styles. Their paintings are very individual but all are simplified. The French artist Henri Rousseau (AD1844/1910), seen above, is a famous example of a Primitive painter.

Acknowledgements

Page 3: Copy of an Egyptian wall painting from the tomb of Menne at Thebes, showing the assessment of crops. Reproduced by permission of the Trustees of the British Museum.

Page 4: *Toreador,* Cretan wall painting from the Palace at Knossos. Heraklion Museum. Photo: Scala.

Page 6: Illuminated pages from the Lindisfarne Gospel. Cotton MS Nero D.iv, fol. 26v and 29. Reproduced by permission of the British Library.

Page 7: *The Lamentation over Christ* by Giotto. Arena Chapel, Padua. Photo: Scala.

Page 8: (top right) *The Tribute Money* by Masaccio. Brancacci Chapel, Santa Maria del Carmine, Florence. Photo: Scala. (bottom right) *Venus and Mars* by Botticelli. National Gallery, London.

Page 10: (left) *The Marriage of Giovanni Arnolfini and Giovanna Cenami* by van Eyck. National Gallery, London. (right) *Hell* by Bosch. Prado, Madrid. Photo: Scala.

Page 11: (centre right) *Anne of Cleves* by Holbein the Younger. Louvre, Paris. Photo: Cooper-Bridgeman Library. (botton left) *Children's Games* by Breugel. Kunsthistorisches Museum, Vienna. Photo: Cooper-Bridgeman Library.

Page 12: (left) *Portrait of Mona Lisa* by Leonardo. Louvre, Paris. Photo: Scala. (right) *Cartoon: The Virgin and Child with St Anne and St John the Baptist* by Leonardo. National Gallery, London.

Page 13: (right) *The School of Athens* by Raphael. Vatican. Photo: Scala. (left) *The Creation of Adam* by Michelangelo. Detail of the ceiling of the Sistine Chapel, Vatican. Photo: Scala.

Page 14: *Madonna of the Long Neck* by Parmigianino. Uffizi Gallery, Florence. Photo: Scala.

Page 15: *The Emperor Charles V* by Titian. Prado, Madrid. Photo: Scala.

Page 16: *The Supper at Emmaus* by Caravaggio. National Gallery, London.

Page 17: (left) *Battle of the Amazons* by Rubens. Alte Pinakothek, Munich. Photo: Cooper-Bridgeman Library. (right) *Maids of Honour* by Velazquez. Prado, Madrid. Photo: Scala.

Page 19: *Self-portrait aged 34* by Rembrandt. National Gallery, London.

Page 20: *The Swing* by Fragonard. Reproduced by permission of the Trustees of the Wallace Collection, London.

Page 21: (left) *The Oath of the Horatii* by David. Louvre, Paris. Photo: Cooper-Bridgeman Library. (top right) *The Morning Walk* by Gainsborough. National Gallery, London.

(centre right) *Three Ladies Adorning a Term of Hymen* by Reynolds. Tate Gallery, London. (botton right) *The Marriage Contract* (from *Marriage à la Mode*) by Hogarth. National gallery, London.

Page 22: (left) *Officer of the Chasseurs Charging* by Géricault. Louvre, Paris. Photo: Musees Nationaux. (centre right) *Death of Sardanapalus* by Delacroix. Louvre, Paris. Photo: Scala. (bottom right) *The Execution of the Rebels on 3rd May 1808* by Goya. Prado, Madrid. Photo: Scala.

Page 23: (centre right) *Rain Steam and Speed—the Great Western Railway* by Turner. National Gallery, London. (top left) *The Haywain* by Constable. National Gallery, London.

Page 24: (left) *The Luncheon Party* by Manet. Louvre, Paris. Photo: Scala. (right) *Impression, Sunrise* by Monet. Louvre, Paris. Photo: Scala. © S.P.A.D.E.M.

Page 25: (centre left) *The Chair and the Pipe* by van Gogh. Tate Gallery, London. (centre right) *Still-life with Plaster-cast* by Cézanne. Courtauld Institute Galleries, London. (bottom left) *A Young Woman Holding a Powder-Puff* by Seurat. Courtauld Institute Galleries, London. (bottom right) *Nevermore* by Gauguin. Courtauld Institute Galleries, London.

Page 26: (left) *Fruit, Dish, Bottle and Guitar* by Picasso. National Gallery, London. © S.P.A.D.E.M.

(right) *André Derain* by Henri Matisse. Tate Gallery, London. © S.P.A.D.E.M. (bottom left) *Composition with Red, Yellow and Blue* by Mondrian. Tate Gallery, London. © S.P.A.D.E.M.

Page 27: (top left) *Time Transfixed* by Magritte. Art Institute of Chicago. © A.D.A.G.P. Photo: John Webb. (top right) *Mr & Mrs Clark and Percy* by Hockney. Tate Gallery, London. © the artist, courtesy Petersburg Press. (bottom right) *Whaam!* by Lichtenstein. Tate Gallery, London.

Page 28: *The Three Younger Sons of Shah Jahan.* Victoria and Albert Museum, Crown Copyright.

Page 29: Landscape painting Photo: Cooper-Bridgeman Library.
Fishing net and Fuji by Kuniyoshi. Colour woodcut. Victoria and Albert Museum, Crown Copyright.

Page 19: *The Night Watch (The Militia Company of Captain Frans Banning Cocq)* by Rembrandt. Rijksmuseum, Amsterdam. Photo: Scala.

Colours

All paints are made up of three parts: coloured powder called pigment; a medium or binder such as gum, egg or oil, to make it sticky; and a diluent such as water or turpentine to make it liquid.

The pigments which give the paints their colour were originally made from things found in the natural world, such as earth, metals, plants and animals. Now many of them can be manufactured in factories from chemicals as well.

This page shows you some common colours made from natural pigments, and tells you where the pigment comes from.

Indigo. Originally made from blue dye extracted from plants of the Indigofera family.

Rose Madder. Made from a red dye obtained from the roots of a climbing plant called Madder.

Carmine. Made from the dried bodies of the female of a certain type of insect, found on cacti in Mexico.

Purple. Made from a type of shellfish called purpura. This was first discovered by the Greeks and Romans.

Sepia. Made from an inky substance given out by cuttle-fish to confuse their enemies.

Gamboge. Made from gum obtained from various trees which grow in East Asia.

Vermilion. Made from a mineral found in the ground called cinnabar.

Ultramarine. Made from a semi-precious stone called lapis lazuli.

Yellow ochre. Made from clay mixed with a mineral. Ochre can produce colours varying from light yellow to deep brown.

Raw Sienna. Made from earth of the type found in the area near Sienna in Italy. Burnt Sienna is a more reddish-brown.

Raw Umber. Umber is a brown earth. It may have got its name from the Italian word *ombra* which means shadow.

Verdigris. Made from the bluish green substance which forms on copper or brass, when it corrodes.

STORY
OF
MUSIC

Contents

Music in the Ancient World

The story of music goes back to prehistoric times and we can only guess at how it began. Even before people started making instruments, they made music, probably by singing, clapping or hitting things. Most experts agree that people first made music for magical or religious reasons, and it has had an important place in religion ever since. By the time the first great civilisations of the Ancient World had emerged, a great variety of musical instruments were already in use.

This is a whistle made in France about 20,000 years ago, from a piece of reindeer horn. Perhaps it was used to copy bird-songs.

1 Egyptian musicians

Harp Lyre Double reed-pipe Lute

In Egypt many of the royal musicians were women and they were often buried near the royal tombs. Music was involved in every part of life. Dancers and flute players accompanied work in the fields and the treading of the grapes. Here you can see the sort of instruments the Egyptians played.

Hand-held harp

Most of the evidence for musical activity in the Ancient World comes from pictures. This one dates from about 4000 years ago and shows musicians in the ancient country of Sumer.

Assyrian captives

Lyres

In most ancient civilisations, musicians were thought very important, second only to the kings and priests. This was especially true in Assyria. When their army captured an enemy city, they always spared the lives of the musicians.

Flute

Sistrum

Music was also important in temple ceremonies. Here flutes and sistra (a kind of rattle) are being played. Silver and bronze instruments, like trumpets, were used mainly by the army.

Greek music

Choir singing a dythyramb.

It is from the Ancient Greeks that we get the word "music". They called it *mousike,* after the nine muses, goddesses of inspiration.

The Greeks attached great importance to music. Each year in Athens a singing competition was held. Every district formed a choir and sang a *dythyramb,* which was a kind of hymn. People wore special costumes and there was dancing as well. The Greeks also used songs in their plays. These were performed at festivals in honour of the god Dionysius.

This vase painting of a music lesson shows some of the instruments used by the Greeks. Most of these came from the Middle East. The main ones were the harp, or lyre, which they called a kithara, and a reed pipe, called an aulos.

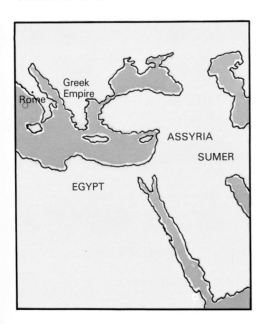

Music in the Roman Empire

Trumpet

Cymbals

In Rome, as in Greece, plays were accompanied by music and so were the gladiator fights. Trumpets and cymbals were used, as shown here, and also pipes, drums and organs.

Jugglers and acrobats performed in the city streets with people playing pipes and tambourines.

Kithara

Wealthy people held concerts in their villas. These musicians are playing pipes and a Roman version of the kithara.

Singers gave big public concerts and were often very well paid. The Emperor Nero, who sang and played the kithara, gave a concert at the theatre in Pompeii in AD65. The next year he toured Greece as a singer. Here he is giving a concert.

Music of the Middle East

The music of the Middle East developed from the traditions and instruments of the ancient civilisations of the area, and so sounds very different from that of Europe. As in Africa and the Far East, the music is accompanied by an instrument which provides the rhythm. The tune is often made up of five basic notes and the sound is varied by putting lots of extra notes between the main ones, so the music sounds as if it is sliding about the scale.

Music has never played a very important part in the Muslim religion, which is followed all over the Middle East, as it was banned by the prophet Muhammad, who founded the religion. However from about the 8th century, music played a major part in life at the courts and palaces of rulers, like the Sultan of Baghdad, shown here.

The music of the Arab peoples today sounds very much as it always has done. The tune is provided by a wind instrument or a singer, while the rhythm is played by the drums. There is usually a rebab, an ud or a tunbur accompanying them as well. Although there are often several players, there are no orchestras in the western sense.

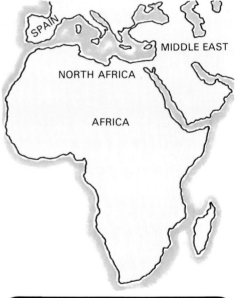

1 The influence of Arab music in Europe

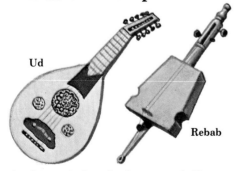

Arab music has had a great influence on European music. After the Crusades, minstrels brought back instruments they had heard, such as the ud and rebab, which became called the lute and rebec.

2 Between the 8th and 15th centuries, Arabs from North Africa invaded and occupied large parts of Spain. At Cordova they founded a school of music and now many Spanish dances have Arab sounds in them.

3 Instruments used in Turkish military bands were brought back from the Middle East during the Crusades. Some of these, such as the shawm, became popular in European bands.

African Music

In African villages, music and dancing are part of everyone's life. Every important occasion, such as the birth of a baby, a marriage or a burial, has special music and dancing to go with it.

African music is not written down, it is memorized and passed down from one generation to the next. We only know about the music of the past from clues like this rock painting found in the Sahara Desert.

The people of the kingdom of Benin, in West Africa, left records of the past in the form of bronze plaques. Many of these show musicians, like this drummer, who evidently played an important part in life there.

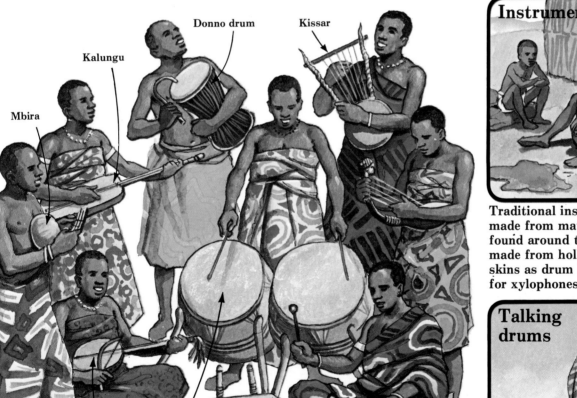

Mbira

Kalungu

Donno drum

Kissar

Atumpan drums

Gondje

Xylophone

Instrument making

Traditional instruments in Africa are made from materials which can be found around the village. Drums are made from hollowed logs with animal skins as drum heads. Gourds are used for xylophones and rattles.

Talking drums

In many African languages words can change their meaning according to how high or low you say them. A drummer can imitate the way Africans speak by altering the tightness of the skin on the drum and by hitting it in different places.

African musicians use a great variety of instruments, especially percussion instruments (ones you hit). The donno drum from West Africa looks like an hour-glass and the atumpan drums are rather like kettledrums. The stringed instruments include a sort of guitar called a kalungu, a harp very similar to the ones played in the ancient world and a lyre called a kissar.

37

Music in the East

The main forms of Indian music can be traced back nearly 2,000 years, to the first chanting of hymns in the Hindu temples. The other countries of Asia and the Far East have a musical history which is just as ancient.

India has a tradition of both folk and classical music. Until quite recently, Indian classical music was played mostly in the palaces of the Indian princes, but now Indian musicians give recitals all over the world.

India

The rules of Indian music are passed down by word of mouth from a *guru* (teacher) to his pupil over many years of study. Its basis is the art of improvisation (making up the music as you go along). The composer provides a set of notes called the *raga* (tune or melody), and the rhythm, called the *tala*. It is then up to the musician to invent the rest of the music around this basic framework provided by the composer.

Vichitra veena · Mirdang · Sarod · Sitar · Tambura · Sarangi · Tabla

Singers and flute players are both popular in India, but stringed instruments, such as the sitar, are more commonly heard. Indian musicians use many more notes than western musicians. To people not used to eastern music, they often sound like western notes played slightly out of tune.

Indonesia

Saron · Gender · Bonang

In Indonesia an orchestra is called a *gamelan*. It often includes singers and colourfully dressed dancers. The word *gamel* means a hammer, and so the *gamelan* is mainly made up of instruments that are hit. The most popular are the gender, the saron (a sort of xylophone), and the bonang (a set of knobbed gongs played with padded sticks). A *gamelan* varies in size, from a few performers, to over 70.

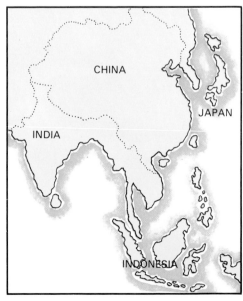

CHINA · JAPAN · INDIA · INDONESIA

China

P'ip'a

Hu ch'in

Very little Chinese music is heard outside China, with the exception of Chinese opera. It can be traced back to the court poetry and folk theatres of at least 1,000 years ago. It has dancing, mime and exotic costumes as well as singing. There are two sets of instruments which accompany the action and singing. The first, for battles and grand entrances, has cymbals, drums, gongs and wind instruments. The second, for quieter scenes, has a small drum, the hu ch'in, which is played with a bow, and the p'ip'a, which is plucked.

Japan

Biwa

Shamisen

The koto

One of the most popular types of Japanese music is the music of the Kabuki Theatre. The players sit on the stage and behind the scenery. They have, among other instruments, the biwa and the shamisen, both kinds of Japanese lutes. The actors wear beautiful costumes. They are all men, even those who are playing women's roles.

One of the most beautiful-sounding of Japanese instruments is the koto. It is tuned by moving bridges under the strings, which are plucked with picks fastened onto the fingers.

The Middle Ages

When the Roman Empire finally collapsed in the 7th century AD, many of the arts that had developed in the Ancient World died with it. But music was kept alive in the churches and monasteries. There were minstrels too, who continued the traditions of the musicians, acrobats and jugglers of the Roman streets. Some wandered from town to town, others were employed by nobles. It was during this period that the present system of writing down music began to be developed.

Much of the church music was sung on its own in a form called plainchant or plainsong. The choir sung a simple tune in unison (everyone singing the same note at the same time). This is often called Gregorian chant, because many of the rules for its use were laid down when Gregory the Great was Pope (AD590/604). Some churches had organs but they were not used much.

When Charlemagne (AD742/815) was crowned as the first Holy Roman Emperor, he invited singers to his court at Aix-la-Chapelle. There composers began to set the words of the Roman poets to music.

Some of these Latin poems were written down by monks with the music to which they were sung. These collections were kept in the monastery libraries.

Musical instruments of the Middle Ages

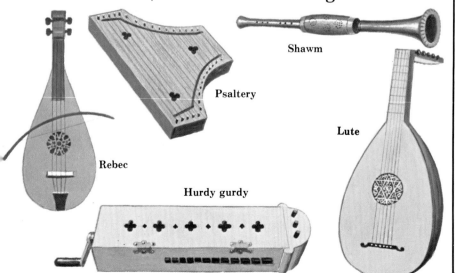

Rebec

Psaltery

Shawm

Lute

Hurdy gurdy

Writing music down

The system of writing music down developed slowly over a long period of time. In the Middle Ages written music looked very different from the way it does now.

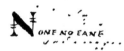

By about the 7th century there was a system that used marks above the words to be sung. The marks were called neumes and they showed the singer roughly how the music went but not the exact pitch and length of the notes.

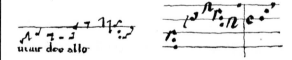

Then people started drawing a line to represent one particular note. Neumes above the line were higher notes, neumes below the line were lower notes. Soon more lines were added. Each line and space stood for a different note. These lines are called a stave or staff.

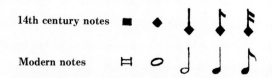

14th century notes

Modern notes

Gradually, as music became more complicated, a system which could show the length of a note was needed, and so shapes were introduced.

Minstrels

Minstrels were the people who sang, played and wrote the non-religious music of the Middle Ages. There were several types of minstrel. Travelling musicians, who often included jugglers and acrobats in their troupes, were called *jongleurs* in France, and gleemen in England.

In France, where there was a long period of peace in the 11th and 12th centuries, noblemen concentrated on writing music and poetry. In southern France they became known as troubadours, in the north as *trouvères*. One of their favourite subjects was the love of gallant knights for beautiful ladies.

Many of these noble poet-musicians were knights who had taken part in the Crusades against the Muslim Turks. One of the most famous was Richard the Lionheart, King of England. The musicians among the Crusaders brought back many musical ideas and instruments from the Arab world.

In Germany the troubadours were called *minnesingers,* which means "singers of love". As the centuries went by their place was taken by the mastersingers, who were usually townspeople. Their guilds held competitions for the best songs. Here you can see a mastersinger, accompanied by musicians.

The "new art"

Landini

Machaut

From about 1300 onwards, some composers started to write much more complicated music. They used more varied rhythms and several lines of melody sung at the same time. This style became known as Ars Nova, which means "new art" in Latin. The most famous centre of this type of music was in Paris, where the great cathedral of Notre-Dame (shown above) was being built.

Some of the composers working at this time are among the first to be remembered by name. Two of the most famous composers of this type of music were Guillaume de Machaut, a French priest, and Francesco Landini, a blind organist from Florence in Italy. Both men were poets as well as musicians, and both composed non-religious songs as well as music to be sung at church services.

Renaissance Music

During the 15th century great changes were taking place in Europe, especially in the way people thought about the world they lived in. New ideas and attitudes affected every area of life—politics, religion, science and, above all, the arts. This period of time is known as the Renaissance.

In music there were several important changes. Church music was still very important but many composers now worked at the courts of wealthy rulers and composed non-religious music as well. People also started to compose music for instruments as well as for voices. But the greatest music of the period was still that written for voices and this vocal music became far more complicated than ever before.

This banquet is at the Duke of Burgundy's court. He ruled an independent province in eastern France. In the 15th century, he employed many of the best musicians in Europe.

The court of the Popes in Rome was another important centre for musicians. Composers, such as Josquin des Près and Giovanni Palestrina, both worked there.

The rulers of England were keen patrons of musicians. King Henry VIII was himself a good composer and musician. He wrote church music, songs and music for dances, like the one above. The reign of his daughter, Queen Elizabeth I, is often thought of as the greatest age of English music, as it produced many of England's best known composers.

Church music

Much of the best music of this time was written for the Church. After the Reformation Protestants started writing music to be sung by the whole congregation, not just by the choir. They also started writing the words in the language of their own country, rather than in Latin. Some musicians continued to write for the Roman Catholic Church.

During the Renaissance madrigals became very popular. These are songs (usually about love) for small groups of voices without any instruments to accompany them.

Madrigals originated in Italy and were performed at all sorts of occasions, especially feasts. This one was to celebrate the wedding of one of the Medici family of Florence.

42

Some famous Renaissance composers

Here are a few of the composers who wrote some of the best music of the Renaissance. Most of them travelled widely in Europe and composed both Church music and non-religious music.

Josquin des Près came from the Netherlands and worked at several courts in France and Italy.

Roland de Lassus came from the Netherlands. He wrote nearly 1,000 works including many Italian madrigals.

The Italian, Giovanni Palestrina, wrote most of his music for the churches of Rome.

Guillaume Dufay came from the Netherlands but worked in France, Italy and Burgundy, composing both church music and songs.

Jean de Ockeghem, also from the Netherlands, was a pupil of Dufay. He worked mainly at the French court.

William Byrd was an Englishman. He was organist at the Chapel Royal and composed mainly church music.

Thomas Tallis was English. He worked with Byrd at the Chapel Royal and shared with him the monopoly of printing music.

Renaissance instruments

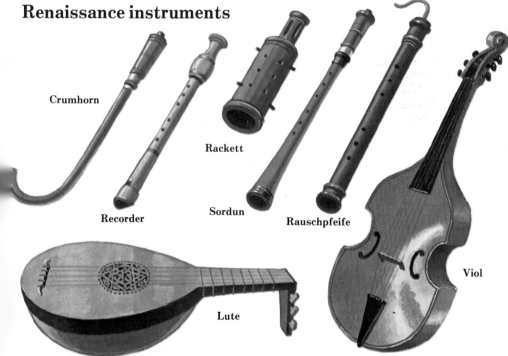

Crumhorn

Recorder

Rackett

Sordun

Rauschpfeife

Lute

Viol

In the Renaissance musical instruments began to be grouped together in sets of four or more. Each instrument in the set covered a different range of notes. If the set consisted of different sizes of the same type of instrument, it was called a consort. Viols, recorders, shawms and racketts all came in different sizes, which were played together as consorts.

Music to listen to

Dunstable (died AD1453)
Ave Marie Stella (song)

Machaut (AD1300/1377)
Notre Dame Mass

Henry VIII (AD1491/1547)
Passtime with good company (madrigal)

Tallis (AD1505/1585)
Spem in Alium (choral work)

Palestrina (AD1525/1594)
Missa Brevis in 4 parts (church music)

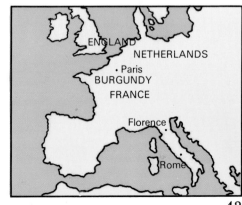

Early Opera and Ballet

In the 17th century, the period called Baroque, music developed into forms which can be more easily recognized today. The way music was printed began to change. The violin became an important instrument for the first time, and keyboard instruments, such as the harpsichord, were used more than ever before. But the furthest reaching new idea of all was opera. One of the first composers of opera was Claudio Monteverdi, whose opera *Orpheo* was first performed in 1607.

Opera in Italy

Venice was an important centre of music at this time. The world's first public opera house opened there in 1637. Many of the great Italian composers worked at St Mark's Cathedral, shown above.

The idea for opera came from a group of poets and composers who met in Florence in the 1590s. They thought that the kind of music used in plays at that time was too complicated and interfered with the stories. So they imagined what a Greek play would have been like, with clear, simple music for the singer and a very simple accompaniment. This new style they called recitative. Above you can see a scene from an early opera.

1 England

One of the most famous English composers of this time was John Dowland. He wrote many songs for the lute, which was the most popular instrument of this period.

2 Lute songs were also used a lot in the theatres, like the Globe in London, where Shakespeare's plays were performed. One of the best composers of these songs was called Robert Johnson.

3 Johnson also wrote music for the court masques of James I and Charles I. These were very expensive entertainments with music, dancing and beautiful moving scenery.

4 The first English opera was performed in 1656, when Oliver Cromwell ruled the country. It was called *The Siege of Rhodes* and this is a design for scenery used in the original performance.

1 The French court

The conductor of Louis XIV's orchestra was Jean Baptiste Lully, who also wrote and performed in many ballets. He died of a poisonous leg after hitting himself with his conducting stick.

Music to listen to

Purcell (AD1659/1695)
Dido and Aeneas (opera)
Ode to St Cecilia
Chaconny in G for strings

Monteverdi (AD1567/1633)
Orpeo (opera)
Vespers of 1610 (church music)

Dowland (AD1563/1626)
Sorrow Stay (song)
Queen Elizabeth's Galliard (lute music)

Johnson (AD1583/1633)
Full Fathom Five (song from the Tempest)

Lully (AD1632/1687)
Grand Divertissements Royal de Versailles

The French court was the most magnificent in Europe. King Louis XIII and his son, Louis XIV were both very musical and made sure that they hired all the best musicians and artists. Louis XIV had an orchestra of 24 violins, which was later copied by Charles II in England. He also studied the guitar and the harpsichord and put on ballets at his palace at Versailles, in which he often appeared himself.

The violin family

Violin

Viola

Cello

Violins were originally instruments for dancing to. In the 17th century, with violas and cellos, they gradually replaced the viol family in serious music.

The harpsichord

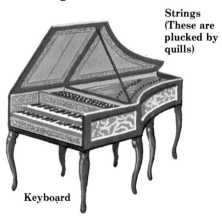

Strings
(These are plucked by quills)

Keyboard

From the 16th to the 18th centuries the harpsichord was the most important keyboard instrument.

Baroque Music

By 1700, several distinct instrumental forms (ways in which the music is arranged and presented) had developed. In the first half of the 18th century these were developed still further. Some of the composers of this period are considered to be among the greatest of any age.

Although music was still strongly associated with the church, music for entertainment was becoming more important, and this period saw the beginning of public concerts.

Antonio Vivaldi lived in Venice, where he was well-known as a violinist. He was a priest, and because of his vivid red hair he became known as "the red priest".

He taught for most of his life at a girls' school, the Pieta. Here his pupils are giving a concert. As well as operas and church music, Vivaldi wrote over 600 concertos.

Pleasure gardens

Throughout the 17th and 18th centuries, there were public performances of music in the various London Pleasure Gardens, such as Vauxhall and Ranelagh.

The idea of a concert, in the sense of a public performance at which an audience pays for the right of admittance, began towards the end of the 17th century.

The concerto

The word "concerto" comes from the Italian word meaning "concert" or "playing together". In the late 17th and early 18th century it was used to describe a piece of music to be played by a small group of solo instruments and an orchestra. A piece like this was called a concerto grosso. Vivaldi, Handel and Bach all composed this type of concerto.

Dance music

Dances were the first kind of music composed only for instruments. In the 17th century, they began to be written together in sets or "suites". The Frenchman, Jean Philippe Rameau, wrote many such dances, both for groups of instruments as part of his ballets, and for the harpsichord. François Couperin also wrote suites for the harpsichord.

Famous violin makers

At this time there were three famous families of violin makers, all working in the Italian town of Cremona. They were the Amati, the Guarneri and the Stradivari. Instruments made in the workshops of these families are very valuable now, especially those of Antonio Stradivari, who is considered one of the greatest instrument makers of all time.

1 Bach

Johann Sebastian Bach came from a family of musicians and grew up with music all around him. He had 20 children of his own, many of whom went into the music profession.

2

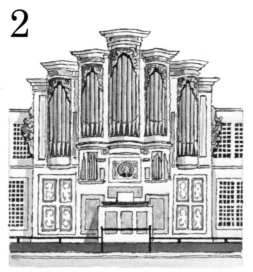

Bach was a very great organist. This is the organ of the church at Arnstadt, which he played when he was organist there. He composed a lot of church music—cantatas, oratorios and passions.

3

Bach also worked at the courts of Weimar, and of Cöthen, where he directed all the prince's singers and musicians. He composed a great deal of chamber music—concertos and suites—to be played at court.

1 Handel

George Frederic Handel was born in Saxony, in Germany. From there he moved to Italy, where he learnt the latest fashions in music. In 1711 he went to London and spent most of the rest of his life in England.

2

Handel wrote many operas. Although his first ones were a success, opera began to lose popularity in England and he found it more and more difficult to find money with which to finance them. So Handel started writing oratorios, such as The Messiah, instead. An oratorio is rather like an opera with a religious theme. It is performed by an orchestra, a chorus and soloists, but without any costumes or action.

3

Handel was a great favourite, both of King George II and his father, King George I. He wrote a lot of music for royal occasions, such as the coronation of George II. George I liked to travel on the River Thames, with boatloads of courtiers in a great procession of barges, and have music playing as he was rowed along. Handel wrote many pieces for this and gathered them together to form *The Water Music.*

Music to listen to

J.S.Bach (AD1685/1750)
The Brandenburg Concertos Nos. 1–6.
Magnificat in D major. (church music)
Jesu, Joy of Man's Desiring.(choral work)
Concerto for 2 Violins and strings in D

J.C.Bach (AD1735/1782)
Symphonies Op.18., Nos. 1–6.

Handel (AD1685/1759)
The Messiah (Oratorio)
The Water Music
Music for the Royal Fireworks

Vivaldi (AD1685/1759)
Concertos Op.8., 1–4, "The Four Seasons",
Gloria in D major (church music)

Classical Music

Although people often call all serious music "classical", the Classical period really refers to the second half of the 18th century. It was then that many of the standard forms of music, such as the symphony, sonata and concerto, were developed. This development can best be seen in the work of Mozart and Haydn.

With the beginning of the 19th century, we move out of the Classical and into the Romantic Age, when musicians extended and further developed the Classical forms.

At this time Vienna was the most important centre of music and most of the famous composers of this period lived or worked there at least for a time.

Music to listen to

Haydn (AD1732/1809)
Symphony No. 100., "The Military"
The Nelson Mass (church music)
The Creation (oratorio)

Mozart (AD1756/1791)
The Magic Flute (opera)
Piano Concerto No. 20 in D minor
Serenade in G., "Eine Kleine Nachtmusik"

Beethoven (AD1770/1827)
Piano Concerto No. 5., "The Emperor"
Symphony No. 9., "The Choral"
String Quartets Nos. 7 & 8.,
"The Rasumovsky"

Schubert (AD1798/1828)
Symphony No. 9., "The Great C Major"
The Trout Quintet
Die Schone Mullern (song cycle)

1 Haydn

For most of his life, Franz Joseph Haydn worked for Prince Esterhazy in Hungary (then part of the Austrian Empire), where he composed a new work nearly every week.

Violins   Viola   Cello

Altogether Haydn wrote 104 symphonies, as well as church masses and music for string quartets (above). A quartet is made up of two violins, a viola and a cello. It is an important

form of chamber music—music originally designed to be played at home. Quartets were very rarely played in public until the middle of the 19th century.

1 Mozart

Wolfgang Amadeus Mozart was only six when he gave his first concert and played for the Emperor, Francis I, in Vienna. At nine, he wrote his first symphony. Here he is with his father and sister.

Writing music was never difficult for Mozart. Although he was only 35 when he died, he still managed to write 41 symphonies and 27 piano concertos, as well as some of the world's most famous operas.

Mozart set some of his operas in his own time, breaking away from the traditional setting of Ancient Greece or Rome. *The Marriage of Figaro*, put on in 1786, was thought daring, as it criticized noblemen.

1 Beethoven

Ludwig van Beethoven was among the first of the Romantic composers. He was also a great pianist and played all five of his piano concertos at their first performances.

2

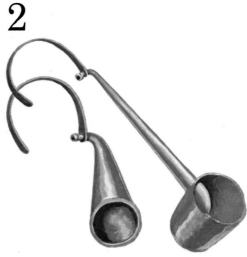

In his 30s Beethoven began to go deaf, but he went on composing until his death about 20 years later. Here are some of the ear trumpets he used to help him hear.

3

Beethoven wrote nine symphonies. In his ninth he included singers and a chorus in the last movement. Before this symphonies had only used the instruments of the orchestra.

The Classical symphony

The word "symphony" means "sounding together" and was first used in the 17th century to describe almost any kind of music for instruments, as opposed to music for voices. By the 18th century "symphony" meant a large scale work for an orchestra and by the end of the century what is known as the "Classical symphony" had appeared.

A Classical symphony usually has four "movements" or sections:
1. A fairly fast, lively movement.
2. A slow movement.
3. A minuet and trio.
4. A fast, cheerful movement.

The Classical concerto

The Classical concerto grew out of the concerto grosso* of the first half of the 18th century. It has a single soloist (instead of a group of soloists, as the concerto grosso had) and consists of three movements:
1. A serious movement. This begins with the orchestra playing alone; the soloist joins in a bit later.
2. A slower movement.
3. A fast movement.

Often a "cadenza" is included towards the end of the first, or last movement, or in both. This is played by the soloist alone, unaccompanied by the orchestra.

The Classical sonata

Sonata originally referred to any piece of music that was played rather than sung. During the 17th and early 18th centuries it was used to describe various kinds of musical composition. By the middle of the 18th century the Classical sonata had emerged.

Classical sonatas are either for a single keyboard instrument, or for a keyboard instrument and one other instrument. They usually have four movements arranged as follows:
1. A long, quick movement.
2. A slow movement.
3. A minuet and trio.
4. A quick and lively movement.

Schubert

Franz Schubert was a young contemporary of Beethoven, from Vienna. Besides symphonies he wrote many songs, or *lieder,* as they are called in German. Here he is playing one of his songs to his friends.

Pianos

Square piano (rarely seen nowadays)

Upright piano (made for playing at home)

Grand piano (usually found in concert halls)

The real name for a piano is a pianoforte, which means "soft-loud" in Italian. It was invented in 1710 in Italy, and became very popular in the Classical period. The difference between pianos and earlier keyboard instruments is that the strings are hit with hammers, instead of being plucked. The harder you strike the keys the louder the notes sound.

*See page 46

The Orchestra

Orchestras developed gradually out of the court bands of the 17th century. Instruments were constantly being improved and new ones added. By about 1830 the modern orchestra was more or less complete. There are usually between 70 and 100 musicians, depending on the music to be played, and there are sometimes soloists and a chorus as well.

Here you can see the main instruments and the way they are usually arranged in the orchestra.

Brass

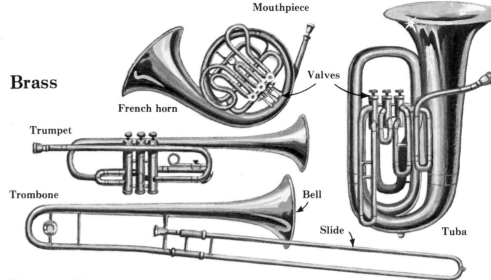

The early 19th century was a great period of mechanical invention, in musical instruments, as in other areas. The greatest improvement in brass instruments was the invention of the valve. Valves, when pressed by the players fingers, bring into use extra lengths of tubing, as well as the main tube, making it possible to play all the notes of the scale. The longer the tube of a brass instrument is, the lower the notes it can play.

Woodwind

Wind instruments, like those above, became gradually easier to play throughout the 18th and 19th centuries. Keys (levers to open and close the holes mechanically) were added so that players could find the notes much faster and more accurately.

Percussion

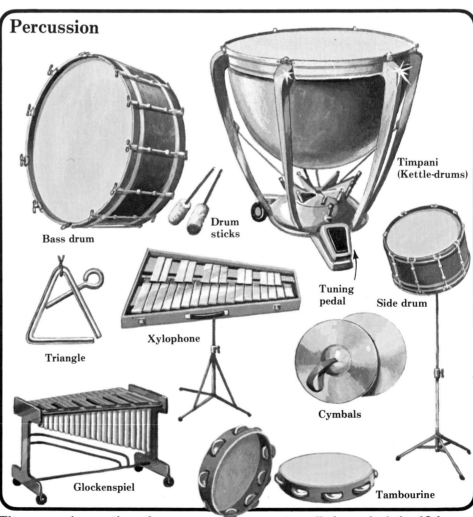

The percussion section of an orchestra can include any instrument which produces a sound when you hit it. In the Classical and early Romantic periods composers rarely used more than the timpani. It was not until the end of the 19th century that percussion became used on any large scale. In the 20th century it has become more and more important and is now often one of the largest sections.

These are the instruments of the string section, drawn to scale. For more information see page 45.

Strings

Violin

Viola

Cello

Double bass

Percussion

Brass

Woodwind

Violas

2nd violins

Harp

1st violins

Conductor

Cellos

Double basses

This picture shows a typical seating plan for a standard orchestra. The different families of instruments—strings, woodwind, brass and percussion—are grouped together. This basic arrangement has existed since the 19th century. Some conductors put the second violins where the cellos are in this picture. If there is a solo part the soloist is put on the left of the conductor.

Concert halls

The first concert halls were built towards the end of the 18th century. Now most big cities have one and many of them have seating for over 3,000 people.

1 The conductor

The conductor was originally a leading member of the orchestra, who used a violin bow, a roll of music or conducted from a keyboard instrument to keep the orchestra in time.

2

Now a conductor uses a finely balanced stick called a baton. He has to decide how fast the music should go and how loud or soft each part should be played.

The Romantics

The 19th century Romantic movement influenced all the arts. In music, composers now wanted to express their feelings and emotions. Beethoven and Schubert led the movement out of the Classical period and into the Romantic. This movement was carried further by the composers on these two pages. Paris and Vienna were Europe's main centres of music at this time. Public concerts became more popular, especially those with music for piano or orchestra.

Two of the most famous musicians of this period were Frederic Chopin, who was Polish, and Franz Liszt, a Hungarian. Both were brilliant pianists and composers of piano music, and both spent much of their lives in Paris. Liszt developed the "symphonic poem", a one-movement piece of music for orchestra, which tells a story. Chopin based much of his music on dances, such as the mazurka, the waltz and the polka.

Programme music

Programme music is any piece of music which tells a story or describes a scene, explained in a written programme. Below you can see four scenes from the story described by the *Symphonie Fantastique,* written by Hector Berlioz.

Berlioz falls in love with a woman. Everywhere he goes her face appears to him. Here he is at a ball, dreaming about her.

Even in the quiet countryside he cannot stop thinking about her, fearing that she is deceiving him.

He tries to kill himself by taking opium. He dreams he has murdered her and is watching his own execution.

In his dream, ghosts, sorcerers and monsters, joined by his beloved, surround him for the funeral.

This is Robert Schumann with his wife, Clara. Schumann was a composer of Romantic piano music. He also wrote songs and symphonies and was a music critic and journalist. Clara was one of the best pianists of her day. In his early 30s, Schumann began to go mad, and he died when still quite young.

The German, Felix Mendelssohn, was one of the most popular and successful composers of the 19th century. He was also famous as a conductor.

Mendelssohn was especially popular in England, where he was a great favourite of Queen Victoria. Here he is being presented to her.

The Viennese court

Johannes Brahms came from northern Germany, but lived in Vienna for the later part of his life. His music continued and developed the style established by Beethoven.

Anton Bruckner settled in Vienna in 1868 and was appointed court organist. He was a very religious man and wrote much music for use in church, as well as nine symphonies.

In the 19th century, Vienna was the capital city of the great Austro-Hungarian Empire, and the Viennese court was the most glittering in the world. It was a very lively place, where people loved to give dances and parties, each more spectacular than the last. For this they needed music. The favourite dances were the polka and, above all, the waltz. There were many composers writing these, but the most famous were a father and son, both called Johann Strauss.

Tchaikovsky

Peter Ilyich Tchaikovsky was one of the first Russian composers to become internationally famous and his music has remained very popular. He wrote symphonies, concertos, operas and three famous ballets. Above is a scene from his ballet *Swan Lake*.

The Austrian composer, Gustav Mahler, also wrote nine symphonies. They need huge orchestras to play them and sometimes a big choir as well. He was a very talented conductor.

Opera

Almost all the most popular operas in the world today, apart from those of Mozart, were written during the last two centuries. In the 19th century operas became full of exciting action, spectacular costumes and scenery and flamboyant music. Operas of this period are often referred to as Grand Opera. During this time many people began to regard opera as the best way of uniting all the arts. Composers like Wagner and Verdi, and, in the 20th century, Britten and Janáček, saw opera as the most important part of their work. Until about 1850 almost all opera was in Italian, but from then on composers usually wrote the words in their own language.

1

Jenny Lind

Luigi Lablanche

In Italy, the music and singing mattered more than the story of an opera. Leading opera singers became very famous and were often angry if they were not given parts that allowed them to show off their voices. As a result composers wrote in a style known as *bel canto*, which means "beautiful singing". Above are two famous singers of the 19th century.

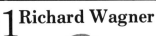

1 Richard Wagner

The German composer, Richard Wagner, believed that the story and the way it was told were as important in opera as the music. He thought that opera could be the greatest form of artistic expression, but felt that there were no opera houses which could stage his operas as he wanted them. With the help of King Ludwig II of Bavaria (shown above), he raised enough money to

2

3

Guiseppe Verdi was the most important composer of 19th century Italian opera. He continued the *bel canto* tradition, with dramatic stories, and tunes which were easy to remember. Verdi wrote 19 operas altogether. They cover a wide range of subjects. The scene above is from *Rigoletto*, which tells the tragic story of a hunchbacked court jester.

have one built to his own design. It is the opera house at Bayreuth in Germany. Every year a festival of Wagner's work is held there. His greatest work was a series of four operas, based on stories from German myths, called *The Ring of the Nibelungs*, which was first performed in 1876. It lasts nearly 20 hours and took him 20 years to write.

4

Giacomo Puccini followed in the tradition of Verdi, and after Verdi's death in 1901, Puccini became the leading Italian composer of opera. This scene is from *Madame Butterfly*, which is about a Japanese girl and an American sailor. This, and another of Puccini's operas, *La Bohème*, are two of the most popular of all operas because of their sad stories and flowing tunes.

1 20th century opera

Richard Strauss was a great admirer of Wagner. He too composed complex operas which need large orchestras. They vary from the lurid *Salome* (above) to the romantic *Der Rosenkavalier* (Cavalier of the Rose).

Leos Janáček, who was a Czech, was one of the most inventive composers of opera. This scene is from *The Cunning Little Vixen*, about a fox. Some of his other works, like *Jenufa*, are about ordinary village people.

Another classic of this century is *Wozzeck*, by Alban Berg. It is about a soldier in the Austrian army. It uses *sprechgesang* (speech-song), a half-speaking, half-singing style, developed by Arnold Schönberg.

Opera houses

The earliest opera houses were built in the 17th century, in big European cities like Venice, London, Paris, Rome and Berlin. In the 18th century many more were built. In Italy and Germany nearly every large town had its own opera house.

In the 19th century composers began writing for much larger orchestras. Bigger theatres were needed, and it was then that many of the world's greatest opera houses were built.

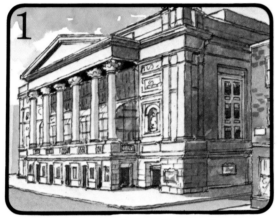

This is the Royal Opera House, Covent Garden, London. It was built in 1858. It is the third opera house to be built on this site. The two previous ones were destroyed by fire.

This is the inside of Milan's famous opera house, La Scala. The first performances of many of the great Italian operas, by composers like Verdi and Puccini, were staged here.

The Vienna State Opera first opened in 1869, but was completely rebuilt after being destroyed during World War II. In 1883 it became the first theatre to install electric lights.

The Sydney Opera House, which opened in 1973, is one of the few great opera houses built in the 20th century. It was designed by a Danish architect called Joern Utzon.

Music to listen to

Rossini (AD1792/1868)
The Barber of Seville
Cinderella

Verdi (AD1813/1901)
Aida
La Traviata

Wagner (AD1813/1883)
The Flying Dutchman
The Mastersingers of Nuremberg

Puccini (AD1858/1924)
Tosca
Turandot

Richard Strauss (AD1864/1949)
Arabella

National Music

In the middle of the 19th century there was much political unrest in Europe. Countries like Germany and Italy struggled to become unified nations, instead of collections of independent states. Many of the smaller countries struggled for independence from the greater ones. This gave rise to a new sense of national identity. In music, composers began looking to the traditions, myths and legends of their own countries for musical ideas.

1 Russia

In St Petersburg*, five composers met to look for Russian stories for their operas and symphonic poems. The group—Balkirev, Mussorgsky, Borodin, Rimsky-Korsakov and Cui—were known as the "Mighty Handful".

2

Rachmaninov composed music in the Romantic style. He left Russia soon after the Revolution and finally settled in the U.S.A., but remained deeply attached to his homeland. He was also a very great pianist.

Folk-song and folk-dance

When composers started wanting to create national styles, they began to take an interest in folk music—unwritten music found mainly in country areas.

Czechoslovakia

Smetana and Dvořák both worked to set up a Czech national style of music, making use of Czech legends, folk songs and dances. Here is a scene from Smetana's opera *The Bartered Bride.*

Hungary

In the 20th century, Zoltán Kodály toured Hungary collecting folk songs that would otherwise have died out. He and Bartók used the rhythms and tunes as a basis for many of their works.

Finland

Finland had hardly produced any composers at all, until Jean Sibelius. He wrote seven symphonies which perfectly captured the feeling of his country's bleak lakes and forests.

Norway

In Norway, Edvard Grieg, wrote about the mountains and fjords. One of his best known works is the music he wrote for *Peer Gynt,* the play by his friend, Henrik Ibsen.

1 England

In England, Ralph Vaughan Williams and Gustave Holst went on walking tours in the countryside, often noting down old local songs. England had had very few notable composers for almost 100 years and they became the centre of a great revival of English music. They were particularly interested in the music of the great Tudor Age.

France

In France, music developed together with the Impressionist movement in painting. Debussy and Ravel were the main composers. Above is a programme design for Debussy's ballet *L'Après-Midi D'Un Faune.*

Edward Elgar was the first important figure in this revival of English music. The success of his *Enigma Variations,* which was performed all over the world, gave new confidence to other English composers.

Frederick Delius is best known for his descriptive orchestral pieces, such as *Brigg Fair,* based on a Lincolnshire folk song. He spent most of his life abroad. Here he is at his home at Grez-sur-Loing, France.

America

Dvořák helped Americans to look to their own past, particularly their negro heritage, for musical inspiration. Charles Ives and later George Gershwin also showed how it could be used in classical music.

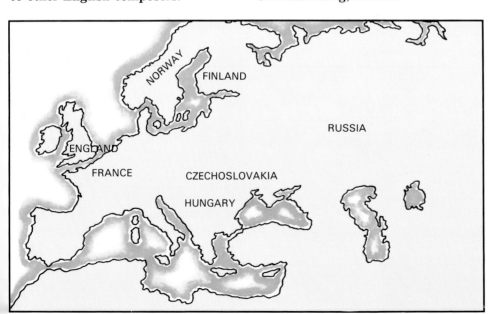

Music to listen to

Rimsky-Korsakov (AD1844/1908)
Scheherazade (symphonic poem)

Mussorgsky (AD1839/1881)
Pictures at an Exhibition (suite)
Nursery Songs

Rachmaninov (AD1873/1943)
Piano Concerto No. 2

Dvořák (AD1841/1934)
Symphony No. 9, "The New World"
Serenade in E for strings

Elgar (AD1857/1934)
Pomp and Circumstances Marches 1–5
Symphony No. 1 in A flat

Vaughan Williams (AD1872/1958)
Greensleeves Fantasia

Operetta and Musicals

Operetta is similar to opera, except that the stories are always amusing. The tunes are catchier and most of the words are spoken rather than sung. It became popular in the Western World from about 1850 onwards.

The musical has developed in the 20th century from a combination of operetta and Music Hall.

In Paris, Jules Offenbach put this high-kicking dance called the can-can, in his operetta, *Orpheus in the Underworld*. The dance was very popular, but some people were shocked.

In England, the writer, Gilbert, and the composer, Sullivan, used operetta to make fun of opera and society. This scene is from *Iolanthe,* where they mock the House of Lords.

The Merry Widow by Franz Lehár is typical of the more romantic operettas of Vienna. It was this tradition that influenced the American musicals of the 1930s and 1940s.

Kurt Weill based *The Threepenny Opera* (1928) on music played in nightclubs. He used actors who could sing, rather than singers, and this became one of the main differences between musicals and operettas.

Music played an important part in the early cinema. The first talking picture, *The Jazz Singer* (1927), was a musical, as were many of the films that followed it. The stories were romantic fantasies, or comments on events of the time. They often included dancing too. Among the most spectacular were the musicals made by the dance director, Busby Berkeley. This scene is from his musical, *The Ziegfeld Girl.*

By World War II, musicals with present day themes became more popular. *Oklahoma!,* a story set in the American countryside, opened in 1943. It ran in New York for five years, with 2,212 performances.

Dance became even more important in musicals such as *West Side Story* (1957). It was a bit like an opera, as the story was tragic, and the music was composed by the classical musician, Leonard Bernstein.

The 1970s saw the arrival of the rock opera—rock music with a story. The first was *Tommy* by The Who. Several others followed. *Jesus Christ Superstar* (above) is probably the most successful.

Jazz

Jazz is a kind of music that developed in America in the last years of the 19th century. The music is not usually written down but is "improvised" by the players. This means that the players start with a musical idea and extend and develop it as they go along.

It has had a great influence on both classical and pop music and lies somewhere between the two. It was at its most popular in the 1930s and 1940s.

Jazz can be traced back to the songs sung by the black slaves, who had been brought over from Africa to work on the plantations in the southern states of the U.S.A., in the 19th century.

In 1866 slavery was abolished and many ex-slaves moved to southern cities, like New Orleans. There they formed their own town bands, which played marches and dances in the streets, especially for funerals.

These musicians also started playing in the bars of New Orleans. Their bands usually included a rhythm section (a string bass, guitar, banjo or piano) as well as brass instruments.

One early type of jazz is called ragtime and is usually played on the piano. Here is the cover of one of the rags written by the pianist and composer, Scott Joplin.

The "Jazz Age" really began after World War I. In the 1920s radio, records and films helped to make it internationally popular, and Chicago became its new centre. In the 1930s and 1940s the best players went to New York and Big Bands and Swing Bands (above), with band leaders like Duke Ellington, Count Basie and Benny Goodman, became all the rage.

Louis Armstrong

Because jazz is usually improvised music, players are really more important than composers. The trumpeter Louis Armstrong was one of the greatest of all jazz musicians.

Duke Ellington

Duke Ellington was a pianist and band leader. Unlike most jazz composers, he wrote his compositions down, but he managed to keep the feeling that it was improvised.

Saxophones

Mouthpiece with reed like a woodwind instrument.

Metal tube, like a brass instrument.

The saxophone was invented by a Belgian instrument maker, called Adolphe Sax, in about 1840. It was adopted by early jazz musicians and became one of the most important ingredients in jazz bands.

Popular Music

In the Western world a lighter kind of music has always existed alongside the more serious classical music. This kind of music is much more closely related to everyday life than classical music, and is called "popular" music, which means "music of the people". It includes folk-songs and dances, traditional ballads, work songs and all the different types of music that have become known as "pop".

Folk-songs

Many folk-songs and folk-dances originally celebrated a particular festival or time of year, like May Day, Christmas or the coming of spring. No-one knows when most of them were composed.

Work-songs

Sea shanties, railway songs and negro work-songs were all made up by people who did heavy work. They used strong rhythms, and often had one part for the gang leader and a chorus for the rest of the gang.

Music Hall

During the 19th century, many people moved to the cities in search of work. The owners of the bars where they went to drink started employing singers and entertainers. Soon, special theatres called Music Halls were built for this kind of entertainment, which also became known as "variety" or "vaudeville" Songs sung in Music Halls were the big hits of the day.

Radio broadcasting

Radio broadcasting began in the 1920s. Songwriters and singers now had the opportunity of getting their songs heard by much larger audiences and of becoming very famous. One of the most successful of the early radio stars was the singer, Bing Crosby.

Gramophones and records

In the 1920s gramophones and records became widely available and people started to have them in their homes. The records were made of a substance called shellac, which broke very easily. They played at a speed of 78 revolutions per minute, each side lasting about four minutes. The first really popular ones were of dance music, like the charleston.

1 Pop music

In the 1950s, rock n' roll became wildly popular with young people all over America and later in Europe. Elvis Presley was the most successful of a series of rock n' roll solo singers.

In the early 1960s pop music in England began to be played by "groups", usually consisting of lead, rhythm and bass guitarists and a drummer. The Beatles were the first group to become world-famous.

Pop music was spread to huge audiences by television, film, radio and records. This meant that live performances also attracted large audiences. In the late 1960s and early 1970s huge outdoor music festivals were held. Recent developments in sound equipment meant that the music could be heard over large distances.

Singers like Bob Dylan, used a mixture of folk-song and rock styles to write and sing "protest" songs. Their words are about the injustice they saw in the world around them.

In the 1970s various different styles of pop music came and went. One of these was disco music. With its strong and regular rhythm it brought in a new dancing craze.

1 New inventions

Long playing records (LPs) and singles, made of unbreakable plastic, appeared in the 1950s, followed in the 1960s by stereo recordings, which create a sound much closer to that of live music.

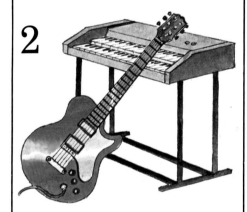

New instruments, like electric guitars, pianos and organs, have been developed and become widely used, and electronic instruments, like synthesizers*, can create totally new sounds.

The quality of sound from recordings of music has been vastly improved by the invention and development of tape recording. Modern recording studios are constantly getting new equipment.

See page 63

Classical Music in the 20th Century

The music of the 20th century includes a great variety of styles. Some composers have continued to use forms like the symphony and concerto, others have created new forms. Percussion instruments have become more important and electronic instruments have helped to create totally original sounds.

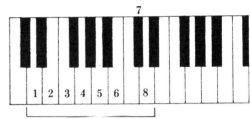

When the ballet, *The Rite of Spring*, by Igor Stravinsky, was first performed in Paris in 1913, it caused a riot. The people in the audience who hated it fought in the theatre with those who thought it was the most exciting music they had ever heard. The ballet is about a primitive Russian folk ritual for the beginning of spring and the music sometimes seems fierce and disturbing compared to earlier ballets.

New directions

From the first years of the 20th century, composers began to break away from the system of music based on eight-note scales (keys), which had been used in Europe since the Renaissance. Very strict rules had developed for the key system and composers wanted something new.

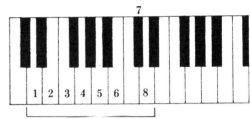

Eight-note scale (octave)

Twelve-note row

An Austrian composer called Arnold Schönberg developed a new system. He used a scale, or row, of 12 notes, using every note between the first and last note of the eight-note scale, instead of just some of them. Music composed using this system is called serial or atonal.

The Rite of Spring was one of the ballets put on by Sergei Diaghilev (above). His Russian Ballet Company in Paris commissioned new works from many of the best composers, including Ravel and Debussy.

Igor Stravinsky was born in Russia, but also lived in France and America. During his life he wrote in several different styles and he had an immense influence over other composers. He died in 1971.

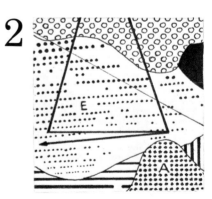

Composers have also experimented with new ways of writing music down, in order to express things that would be very difficult to express using the normal system.

New inventions

Some composers have experimented with new kinds of musical sound. Sometimes they use everyday noises like radios, door-keys or car horns.

Sometimes they alter traditional instruments, for example, by putting drawing pins and rubbers inside a piano, or playing a cymbal with a violin bow.

The invention of the tape recorder in the 1940s made it possible to create a vast new range of sounds by cutting tape, speeding it up, and playing it backwards. Often specially prepared tapes are now used in performance with live musicians.

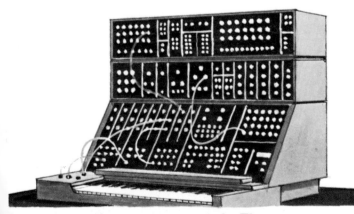

An even newer instrument, the synthesizer, uses a computer to imitate voices, instruments and other sounds. The computer can put them all together to make new sounds of its own.

Some composers of the 20th century

Dmitri Shostakovich wrote 15 symphonies and string quartets, which reflect his sadness at the terrible events happening in Russia in his time.

Olivier Messaien lives in France. He is most famous for his organ music and his piano works, which use the way birds sing as their basis.

Benjamin Britten lived on the coast in eastern England—the setting for his opera, *Peter Grimes*. He also wrote many works for boys choirs.

Witold Lutoslawski is one of Poland's greatest living composers. He uses both traditional musical ideas and modern serial techniques for his works.

Luciano Berio comes from Italy. He is one of the composers who has used electronic instruments and tape recordings in his compositions.

Peter Maxwell Davies is English but lives on one of the islands off the coast of Scotland. Often his music takes its theme from the islands' history.

Music to listen to

Schönberg (AD1874/1951)
Pierrot Lunaire
The Transfigured Night

Stravinsky (AD1882/1971)
The Firebird (ballet)
Pulcinella (ballet)
Symphony of Psalms

Messaien (born AD1908)
L'Ascension (for organ or orchestra)

Shostokovich (AD1906/1075)
Symphony No. 7, "The Leningrad"

Barber (born AD1910)
Adagio for Strings
Essay for Orchestra

Britten (AD1913/1976)
Young Person's Guide to the Orchestra
Ceremony of Carols

Lutoslawski (born AD1913)
Concerto for Orchestra
Les Espaces de Sommeil

Berio (born AD1925)
Sequenza 1 to 9

Maxwell Davies (born AD1934)
The Two Fiddlers (opera)
The Martyrdom of St Magnus (opera)

Index